BAD FROGS

Thacher Hurd

BAD

FROGS

CANDLEWICK PRESS

Bad frogs, green and slimy.

Riding

motorcycles.

Slurping ice cream.

Bad frogs.

Very

bad frogs.

Wearing bad hats. Wearing dark glasses.

Staying up late.

Kissing their girlfriends.

Bad frogs.

Very bad frogs.

Bad frogs.

Riding skateboards.

Chewing newt gum.

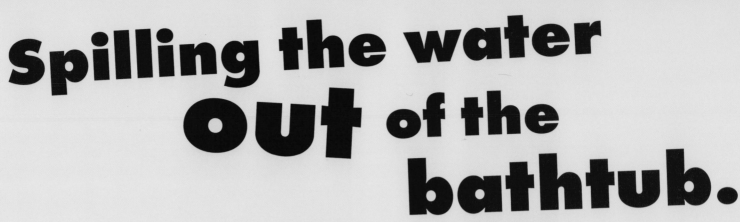

Spilling the water OUT of the bathtub.

Bad frogs.

Very bad frogs.

Could they be good?

Could they be quiet?

Could they dress up in

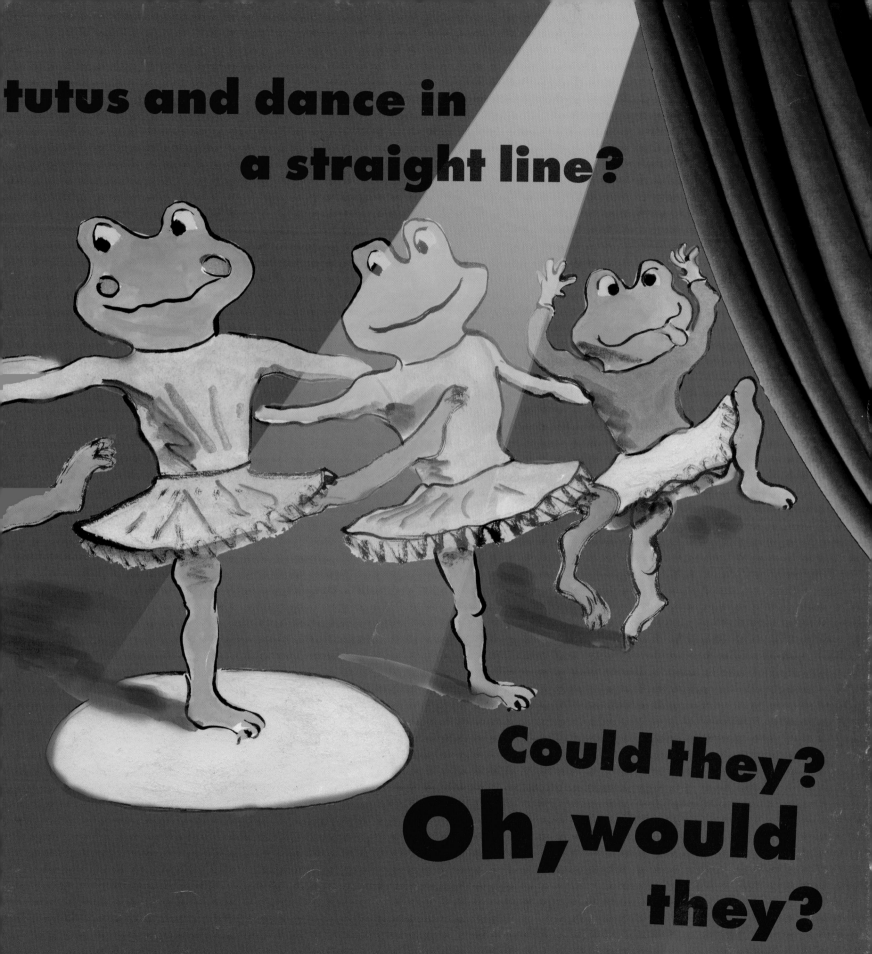

They'll **never** say "Please."

They'll fight with their toothbrushes.

For Manton and Yesica

First U.S. edition 2009

Library of Congress Cataloging-in-Publication Data is available.

Library of Congress Catalog Card Number 2008933128

ISBN 978-0-7636-3253-3

10 9 8 7 6 5 4 3 2 1

Printed in China

This book was typeset in Futura T Extra Bold.
The illustrations were done in watercolor, pencil,
and ink with digital enhancement.

Candlewick Press
99 Dover Street
Somerville, Massachusetts 02144